For my beautiful friend Shiraz,
undisputed Princess of Elephants
and Queen of Hearts

Kids Can Press acknowledges the financial support of
the Government of Ontario, through the Ontario Media
Development Corporation's Ontario Book Initiative; the
Ontario Arts Council; the Canada Council for the Arts;
and the Government of Canada, through the BPIDP,
for our publishing activity.

Published in Canada by
Kids Can Press Ltd.
29 Birch Avenue
Toronto, ON M4V 1E2

Published in the U.S. by
Kids Can Press Ltd.
2250 Military Road
Tonawanda, NY 14150

www.kidscanpress.com

The artwork in this book was rendered in mixed media.
The text is set in Litterbox.
Edited by Tara Walker
Designed by Karen Powers
Printed and bound in China
This book is smyth sewn casebound.

CM 06 0 9 8 7 6 5 4 3 2 1

Library and Archives Canada Cataloguing in Publication

Côté, Geneviève, 1964—
      What elephant? / by Geneviève Côté.

ISBN-13: 978-1-55337-875-4
ISBN-10: 1-55337-875-X

1. Elephants—Juvenile fiction. I. Title.

PS8605.08738W48 2006   jC813'.6   C2005-907047-1

Kids Can Press is a CORUS™ Entertainment company

What elephant?

Written and illustrated by Geneviève Côté

KIDS CAN PRESS

IT was a quiet day, a day like any other day, when George burst out of his front door shouting at the top of his lungs, "Help! Help! There's an elephant in my house!"

A small crowd gathered around George.

"Elephants don't break into houses," someone giggled.

"But this one did — it REALLY did! When I went home there was an elephant sitting on my couch! It was watching TV and eating my chocolate chip cookies!" insisted George.

His best friend, Pip, shook his head. "Elephants don't watch TV, and they certainly don't eat chocolate chip cookies. You were probably out in the sun too long. Why don't you go home and get some sleep?"

"Maybe Pip is right," George said to himself as he slowly walked away.

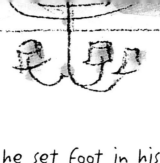

But the minute he set foot in his house, George heard **LOUD** snores coming from the bedroom.

An elephant was sprawled across his bed.

George settled on the broken couch. (Elephants should **NEVER** sit on couches.) And since the elephant had blown its very large nose on every single one of his bed sheets, George covered himself with old newspapers.

"I'll go to sleep, and surely, **SURELY** when I wake up everything will be quite normal," he thought as he closed his eyes.

But when George awoke the next morning, the couch was floating on a sea of soapy water. George heard **LOUD** splashing coming from the bathroom. The elephant was in the shower. (Elephants should **NEVER** linger in showers.)

"When will I wake up from this very strange dream?" George wondered as he fished out his prized collection of teapots.

By the time he had mopped the floor, George
was very hungry.

But when he opened the kitchen cupboards, there
was nothing but crumbs! ALL the cookies and peanut
butter, ALL the bread, milk and bananas were gone.

George heard a loud **BURP** coming from the dining room. (Elephants should **NEVER** eat cookies for breakfast.)

"This must be the longest dream in the whole world," sighed George as he walked to the grocery store.

But when George came back,
the elephant was still there.
    It was sitting on George's broken
couch, reading George's newspaper
and wearing George's dressing gown.
    "Elephants can't read," said George.
"This isn't really happening."

But day after day, the elephant remained. And George just stepped around it. He stayed home and kept to himself. He ate little and slept even less. And he hardly ever smiled anymore.

"Maybe I'm crazy," he worried. But he didn't dare tell anyone about the elephant again, not even Pip.

After a whole week had gone by, Pip came round to inquire after George. "You don't seem like yourself," he said. "I hope you aren't seeing elephants again?"

George pretended to laugh. "Elephants? No, of course not! Why, elephants don't live in houses! They don't sleep in beds or eat chocolate chip cookies, and they certainly don't read newspapers! No, I just needed some sleep, like you said."

But when they walked into the garden, Pip suddenly paled. "George, are you ... are you sure you don't see elephants anymore?"

"Maybe he can tell something is wrong with me," thought George, so he answered, "Not even the faintest shadow of an elephant's tail!"

"Oh, no," thought Pip, "then I'M going mad!" for he could see, right there in the middle of the garden, a large elephant, shiny with suntan lotion.

He felt too embarrassed to tell George.

So George and Pip chatted about the weather. Neither of them mentioned the overpowering scent of coconut oil.

A little later, when their friend Maggie came by, she stopped in her tracks. "Is that an ELEPHANT lounging in the flowerbed?!" she wondered.

But Pip and George didn't seem to notice anything strange.

"This is crazy!" thought Maggie. "I'm seeing things! Maybe I'VE been out in the sun too long."

Determined not to talk about sunbathing elephants, Maggie sat in the shade and stared at her lemonade.

It was such a fine day that many more friends and neighbors stopped by. But each, in turn, fell silent, struck by the same terrible thought: "I must be mad, crazy, nuts, out of my mind!" For no one mentioned, or even seemed to notice, a large elephant lying lazily in the sun.

Suddenly, the silence was broken by a shout: "SHIRAZ! THERE YOU ARE! I've been looking for you all week!"

A very angry little man marched toward George. "You, sir! Why didn't you bring her back? Why did you hide my elephant in your house? Shiraz, my little buttercup, are you all right?"

He flung his arms around the elephant.

"I ... uh ... I tried to ... uh ..." stammered George.

"I ... uh ... I thought ... uh ..." stuttered Pip.

"I ... uh ... I didn't want anyone to think ... uh ..." stumbled Maggie.

Then George and his friends looked up at the elephant right there beside them. They each let out a **HUGE** sigh of relief, struck by the same wonderful thought: "I'm not mad, crazy, nuts or out of my mind after all."

When they began to explain, the little man laughed, wondering how anyone could **NOT** see an elephant!

"You must have thought that you were invisible here, poor cupcake!" Hugging the elephant, he said to the crowd, "She ran away because the circus hired a new talent, and my Shiraz wants to be the only star! My little sweet pea, don't you know you'll always be my **BIGGEST** star?"

And Shiraz dropped two large tears on her trainer's nose.

After lemonade and chocolate chip cookies,
Shiraz and the little man walked off into the sunset,
side by side. (Elephants should **NEVER** leave on an
empty stomach.)

With embarrassed giggles, everyone else drifted
away, and soon George was alone with Pip.

"I'm sorry, George," said Pip. "I should have
believed you from the start."

"And I should have insisted —" George began, when
he was politely interrupted by a high-pitched voice ...

"Excuse me gentlemen, which way is it to the train station?"

Surely, SURELY this couldn't be the voice of a pink poodle carrying a pink suitcase?

"Pip ... Pip, did you hear that?"
"Uh ... hear what?"

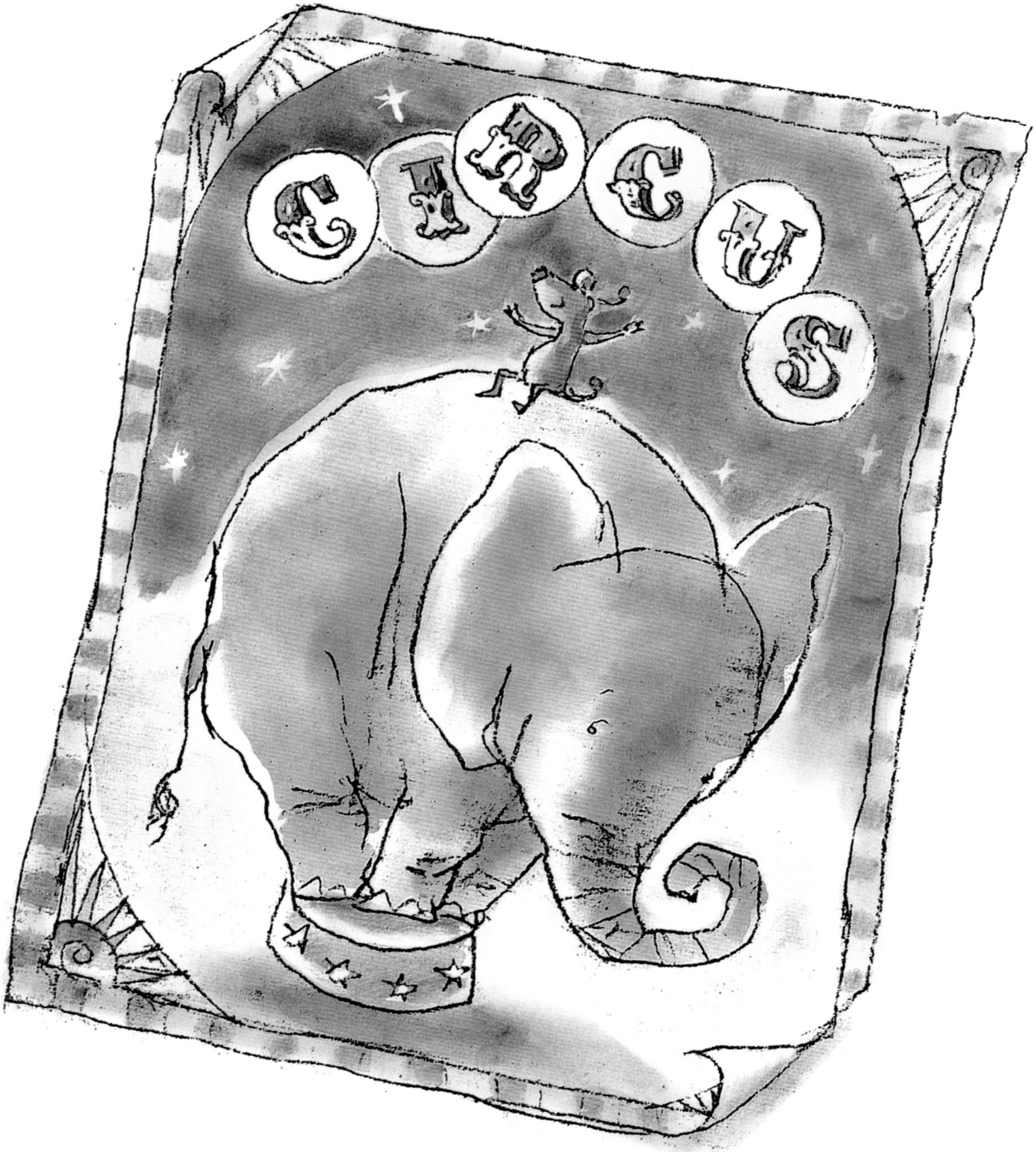
CIRCUS